Anonymous

Scenes in Switzerland

Anonymous

Scenes in Switzerland

ISBN/EAN: 9783337184308

Printed in Europe, USA, Canada, Australia, Japan

Cover: Foto ©Andreas Hilbeck / pixelio.de

More available books at **www.hansebooks.com**

SCENES

IN

SWITZERLAND.

GRETCHEN.

A NIGHT IN THE CATHEDRAL.

THE BRIDE OF THE AAR.

PUBLISHED BY THE
AMERICAN TRACT SOCIETY,
150 NASSAU-STREET, NEW YORK.

SCENES IN SWITZERLAND.

GRETCHEN.

TIME flies swiftly when we are sight-seeing; and it was late in the autumn of 18— when I reached Lindau. Lake Constance lay before me, a pale, green sheet of water, hemmed in on the south by bold mountain ranges, filling the interim between the Rhine valley and the long undulating ridges of the Canton Thurgau. These heights, cleft at intervals by green smiling valleys and deep ravines, are only the front of table-land stretching away like an inclined plane, and dotted with scattered houses and cloistering villages. The deep green of

forest and pasture land was beginning
to show the touch of autumn's pencil;
the bright hues striking against gray,
rocky walls; the topmost edge of each
successive elevation crowned with a
sharp outline of golden light, deepening
the purple gloom of the shaded slopes.

Behind and over this region towers
the Sentis, its brow of snow bristling
with spear points. It was altogether
too late to think of the Baths, or even
to look at the little lake of Wallenstatt;
and still, I was unwilling to return without a friendly shake of the hand of my
old friend Spruner, who had perched
himself in one of the upper cantons.
"You should have been here earlier,"
said the landlord; "in summer we have
plenty of visitors."

"I rather look upon the mountains
in their parti-colored vests, than when
dressed in simple green," I replied.

"If you can stand the weather;" and he thrust his pipe deeper into his mouth, and twirled the button of his coat.

Hastily making my adieus, the postillion cracked his whip, and we started. "There is no danger of bad weather for a month," said the driver, "and when we get up farther you will see what will pay you for the trouble of coming:" a speech that promised well for the day, I argued; and a certain share of respect leaped up for the man in his laced coat and steeple-crowned hat. A good specimen of his class—and once satisfied of this, I gave myself up to the present, without the least foreboding with regard to the future.

Over us hung masses of gray cloud, stretching across the valley like a curtain, and falling in voluminous folds almost to the level of Lake Constance. As we passed through this belt, and came out, with cloud and mist below us, I listened as the postillion related the popular legends handed down from one generation to another, for the last six hundred years. Reaching the crest of the topmost height, he stopped suddenly.

"It is just the day to see the herdsmen;" and he threw down the reins, and prepared to dismount. I stood up and looked around.

"The battle you know between the herdsmen and the monks, with Austria to help. It was a hard battle, and the knights were whipped; and ever since, on certain days, the herdsmen are seen armed with bows and pikes," he continued. By this time I had taken in his meaning, and turning my attention to the misty curtain rolling up into clouds about the sides of the mountain, I had no difficulty in picturing the discomfited

Austrians flying from the pursuit of the hardy mountaineers.

"It was a great battle, and they have never tried it since," and there was a ring in the voice that sounded like the echo of Grütli.

"No wonder, if your herdsmen are still ready to keep up the fight."

"You do not see them," and he made a gesture in the direction where my eye still lingered.

"As plainly as any body can," and I tried hard not to smile.

"It is quite true this;" and he gathered up the reins.

"I do not doubt it."

As we passed on, the clouds rounded into islands, touched with silver on the upper edges.

"This is the place for fine muslin and embroideries," said the postillion in a changed tone.

" Where are they made ?" I asked.

" Every house has a loom," he said.

A small way to manufacture muslins ; but when the density of the population and the incessant labor is taken into consideration, it is not so strange. With regard to the houses I was greatly disappointed. Not only are they so near that neighbors can converse freely, but they are large, and even luxurious, in comparison with the same class in other parts of Europe. Many of these houses are four stories, with large, square rooms at the base ; the upper ones narrowed by the high steeple roof which projects several feet, forming balconies, beautifully carved and highly ornamented. The outer walls are covered with shingles from two to three inches broad, overlapping each other, and rounded at the ends ; reminding one of old roofs seen in the French quarter.

The lowest story is of stone, plastered, and whitewashed. Such a house is very warm, very durable; and painted by the successive changes of winter and summer, the external appearance is altogether pleasing. Our ascent was gradual; with stately houses one after another, and fruit-trees on the sheltered side. In the balconies, pots of bright-hued flowers, and sometimes a face to greet us.

Towards sundown we halted at the little town where my friend had deposited himself; and as my foot touched the wooden step of the little hotel, whom should I meet but my old college chum; no longer thin and pale as when I knew him, but round-faced as an alderman, and merry as though his heart was full of new wine.

"You are not to stop here," as the landlord came out to receive me: "My house is not far off, and GRETCHEN, you remember her? will be glad to see you."

Of course I remembered Gretchen ; but to meet her as my friend's wife was quite another thing. A few steps brought us to the door of a handsome establishment two centuries old, or more ; the front frescoed, and the interior neat and order- ly as a New England housewife's. The floor upon which we entered from the street was paved with a species of mar- ble, black and white, diamond shaped, but too suggestive of cold to be altogeth- er pleasing. A broad, wooden staircase of a peculiar rich brown hue led to the parlor on the second floor. The win- dows looking out into the mountain ran- ges were draped with ruby-colored dam- ask ; the floor was covered with a richly tufted carpet bordered with flowers, and sofas and easy chairs were temptingly arranged. On a table in the centre of the room, and under an elaborately chased lamp, were implements for letter-writing, magazines, and newspapers. Through the folding-doors we caught a glimpse of well-filled book-shelves, and a woman's voice came floating out to the rich, mellow accompaniment of the piano. There was the rustle of a silk dress. I turned my head.

"This is my ambition," said my friend, while a look of pride blended with the manly expression of his handsome face.

There stood Gretchen—the Gretchen I had known ten years before; no longer the slight blushing girl, but mature in her beauty, a happy wife and mother; the same sweet smile on her lips, and her eye full of gushing gladness as she welcomed me to her home.

The fire was blazing cheerily, and we three talking of the old times, with hardly a thought of the broken links between.

"The college is still the same," said my friend, "with the high cupola and long galleries. Gretchen and I visited it last summer; there were few that we knew, and many of the professors have slipped away. Gretchen's father was one of these. We missed him in his quiet home, and above all, in the old church. A man with dark hair and black flashing eyes stood in his place—a learned man, but wanting in the inward fire, the simple eloquence of the old man we used to love. After service, I strolled past the college buildings, and tried to trace the names we cut on the old beeches, but they were all overgrown."

"I know nothing that brings home to the heart so quickly the consciousness of increasing years, as to find those whom we used to look upon as children grown to maturity, taking upon themselves the care and responsibility of life.

Here is Gretchen ; a deeper bloom upon her cheek,-and her eye sparkling with a higher pride."

"Just as mid-day is brighter than the morning," said my friend.

Down the hall came the pattering of little feet, and the nurse entered with two stout boys and a lovely girl, a second Gretchen, the same roguish blue eyes, and golden hair rippling away from her white forehead.

"These are my hopes," said the father, and a smile curled his lip, and his eye filled with tenderness as he glanced at Gretchen's face. Lingering over the tea-table where Gretchen presided with more than youthful grace, we talked not only of the past, but of present work and life.

"One," I continued, taking up the thread, "I met in Southern Italy, dreaming, as I was dreaming, by the dark

grotto of Pausilippo. Meeting upon
classic ground, it seemed strange to talk
of old times, but we did. And sitting
down upon the promontory of Baiæ, looking off upon the blue sea, we told each
other our respective stories; just as ships
will shift their course to come within
speaking distance, compare longitude,
and exchange letters, and—part. I have
not heard from Eckerman since."

My dreams were pleasant that night,
and the next morning there was another
surprise for me. Gretchen's brother was
the pastor of a little church just above
them; I must not go without seeing him,
Gretchen said. How could I? Euler
was my classmate; together we labored
for knowledge, and our first manly sympathies run in the same channel.

On Sabbath I saw my friend in the
pulpit. "How like his father," I whispered to Gretchen; the poetry in him

warming his soul into a burst of fervid eloquence, and his face glowing with the beautiful truths he was unfolding to his hearers. An uncouth church of rough stone, with quaint windows and curious carvings, the ceiling arched, with a blue ground on which blazed innumerable stars. Strange and novel as it was, my eye never wandered from the speaker; the voice and expression so like the kind and generous man who had presided over the college, and who carried with him the affections of each succeeding class. This seems to me more of a triumph now, than it did then. A cultivated mind may challenge respect, but there is need of a noble one to win affection.

It was a week before I could think of leaving, and then the clouds twisted through and around the severed pyramids of the Alps, and the rain began.

In such weather the scenery is not only shrouded, but the people are shut up in their homes. Pastor Euler had an ample study however, and here we read and wrote, and talked; with his wife, a pleasant-voiced woman, to enliven the pauses with music, and children dashing into the study giving abrupt and sudden turnings to our dreaming. Christmas was near, and I was easily persuaded to see more of a people, shut in as they were from the noise and commotion of the lower world, and still not so far as to be unknowing of all that was taking place, whether in deliberative bodies, state policies, or the lighter chit-chat of the day.

"You will have an opportunity to see more of my parish than you can possibly see on a Sabbath occasion. I visit them as often as I can, and twice a year I receive them at my own house. The

'Weihnachtsgeschenk' is looked forward to with great pleasure, and the meeting of the Landsgemeinde in April is sure to bring my people together."

Gretchen and her husband were clamorous for me to remain, and there was no resisting the pleading tones of the children, their little clinging fingers stronger than bands of iron.

All night the rain beat against my chamber window, and in the morning the lower slopes of the mountain were white with new snow. Dark clouds lay heavily on the Alpine peaks, the air was raw and chilly—still it was Christmas. I was aroused at daybreak by the chiming of village bells, and then a procession of choral singers went through the streets, pausing under the window of each house, and singing Christmas hymns. As they passed on, the children caught up the refrain, and joining hands made the halls resound with their gleeful voices. Before breakfast a huge bowl was passed around with a foaming drink, not unlike egg-nog in appearance, but differing in taste materially. "May your Christmas be a merry one," as it passed from lip to lip; "and a profitable one," was always responded.

Church was open an hour earlier than on ordinary occasions, "so that the people may have ample time for dinner," said the pastor. Religion with these mountain worshippers was not a form. The birthday of the blessed Redeemer was to them a reality. They believed that he was born and that he died; and it was to commemorate his nativity that hymns were sung and garlands wound. At an early hour they began to gather, and before the time of service the house was closely packed. There were no chains of evergreen, but small fir-trees were occasionally placed. These were covered with garlands and crowns of bright-hued flowers, giving a novel and striking appearance, as of some floral temple or mosque, set in a great pavilion. The high pulpit was draped in white, and a voluminous white curtain covered the background. The effect was charming.

And as the pastor began the service, the melody of his voice broke away into tenderness as he touched upon the love of God in giving his Son to be the propitiation for sin: holding up the picture so vividly, and telling the simple story with a pathos and a power that little children even could not fail to see and to appreciate. How much better than studied and elaborate essays, diving into metaphysics and technicalities so deeply that beauty is lost, and the mind diverted by the difficulty of following the intricate windings.

First did he impress his hearers with
the fact that God loved the world, and
through the fulness of that love the Son
came down to suffer and to die : second-
ly, that the natural heart is at enmity
with God, not willing that God should
rule. Thus a change must be effected ;
a reconciliation made. This could only
be wrought by sacrifice ; and Christ was
offered once for all ; his blood cleanseth
from all sin. A plain, simple statement,
and it sunk into the hearts of his hearers with a power sure to tell upon their
future lives.   .

After the blessing, each remained
silently upon his knees for a few mo-
ments. Then all was greeting and con-
gratulation ; all were friends ; the idea
never entered their heads that a stran-
ger could be among them at that season.

At dinner I was introduced to the
landamman and two other members of

the council, and from them gathered brief notes with reference to the little democracy won, and held intact for so many years. The dessert was hardly removed before they began to come: first the old men in black coats and high hats, and women with white, pointed caps and wide ruffles; then the middle-aged, fathers and mothers, bringing little children, all with the same conscientious expression on their faces, the same "Happy Christmas," while the pastor's "God bless you," was a benediction that carried happiness to the hearts of . those who heard it.

Lastly came the youths; maidens with eyes full of a childlike innocence, the quick color coming and going as they greeted the pastor and his friends, and received his blessing in return. Gretchen and her husband were with us, and Gretchen number two was my especial escort, leading me through the rooms, and introducing me in her naive manner, "Mamma's friend, and papa's, and uncle Euler's."

Christmas festivities were kept up during the week; and before that elapsed, I was won to add a month, and then another, it being quite impossible to slip away from the kind friends with whom I had so much in common; the fascination only the more potent as we listened to the beating winds, and looked out into the slippery paths leading down into the cantons beneath.

Spring had come when it was "fit to travel," as Gretchen said. The green of the landscape was brilliant and uniform; the turf sown with primrose, violet, anemone, veronica, and buttercups. It was time for me to leave; neither could I be persuaded to stay till the meeting of the Landsgemeinde. It was

sad to leave them, and the little Gretchen was only pacified by my assurance
that, if possible, I would return at no
distant day. My friend Spruner had
business at Herisau, and spending one
more evening together, our prayers
mingling for the last time, we parted.

Our way led through the valley of
the Sitter, a stream fed by the Sentis
Alps, and spanned by a bridge hun-
dreds of feet above the water. The
same smooth carpet of velvet green was
spread everywhere.

"There is no greener land," said
Spruner; "the grass is so rich that the
inhabitants cannot even spare enough
for vegetable gardens. Our tables are
supplied from the lower vallies."

"In our country we should not dream
of making hay in the month of April,"
I remarked, seeing several stout men
already in the field.

"With suitable care they can mow the same field every six weeks," responded my friend. "And it is no doubt this peculiar process that gives such sweetness and splendor of color, seen nowhere else, not even between the hedgerows of England."

The day proved to be neither clear nor rainy: a steel blue sky brougth out the broken peaks of Kasten, while the white shoulders of the Sentis were veiled with a thin, gray suit.

"A month later and we should see the herdsmen," remarked Spruner. "The leader of the herd marches in front with a large bell suspended from his neck by a handsome leathern band; the others follow, some with garlands of flowers and straps of embroidered leather, with milking pails suspended between the horns."

Before nightfall, occasional streaks of

sunshine shot across the mountain. It
did not last, however, and when we
reached our stopping-place, it was rain-
ing below and snowing above us.

The next morning our road dropped
into a ravine, bringing something to admire at every turn. Leaving our course,
we visited the Cascade of Horsfall, the
beauty of which amply repaid us for the
delay it cost. That night we slept at
Herisau, the largest town in the Canton,
and here I was to part with Spruner.
There was no difficulty in reaching the
lower valley. With many shakes of the
hand, and "May God's blessing be upon
you," we parted: one to take the rail-
road to Zurich, the other back to his
household charms, and the work he had
chosen.

A Night in the Cathedral.

Franz Hoffner's father was kappel-meister; and the old cathedral with its grained arches and cloistered aisles resounded with rare music, as the organist took his seat, and run his fingers over the keys with the careless ease of one who knows not only to control, but to infuse something of his own spirit into the otherwise senseless machine before him. Under his inspiration it became a living, breathing form; lifting the hearts of worshippers, and giving them glimpses of what is hereafter to be obtained.

Herr Hoffner was a rare musician; but, alas, musicians are no exception to the rule: the wheel is always turning; one goes up and another goes down. A

new star had risen. Court belles and
beauties grew enthusiastic. The elector's heart was touched; his influence
was asked. "Herr Hoffner has been
here long enough," it was said. There
was a twinge of the electoral conscience.

Herr Hoffner went to his house a
ruined man; and the new favorite, Carl
Von Stein, played upon the keys so dear
to the heart of the old organist.

Herr Hoffner had a wife and two
lovely children; and one would suppose
that he could live in the beautiful cottage the elector had given him, inde-
pendent of the favorite. But no; de-
prived of his old instrument all else was
lost to him. For hours would he sit
before his humble door, heedless of his
wife's entreaties or the childish prattle
of Franz and Nanette; his eye riveted
on the old cathedral, and his hands playing nervously, as though cheating him-

self with the idea he was still at the organ. Then roused by a sudden inspiration, he would rush to the piano and play till his hands dropped from mere exhaustion.

Franz and Nanette loved music, and they could play skilfully, but they were all too young to be of service; and thus they lived cut off from all outward influences befitting their age; loving music above everything else, and yearning for the time when they could go out and win for their father, as he had once done for them.

Years passed. Franz Hoffner was a tall, slight boy, and his father was blind. Sitting at his cottage door he could no longer see the tall towers of the old cathedral, but he could hear the chime of stately bells—and his fingers played on: while Franz and Nanette not unfrequently climbed up the winding stairs, just to beg Herr Von Stein to let them touch the keys their father used to love.

It happened one day the organist went out and left the key in the lock.   Franz entered with the evening worshippers. A nameless feeling seized him.   Urged on by the sudden impulse, he mounted the stairs.   He did not dream of playing, he only thought of the organ as his father's friend; and to seat himself on the stool where his father had so often sat was all he aimed to do.   A moment, and he spied the key; would there be any harm in raising the lid and playing himself?   Herr Von Stein had never denied him.   He grew courageous.   A few chords and Franz forgot that his father would be expecting him; piece after piece was played till his memory could serve him no longer, and then he began to improvise.

All at once heavy shadows were cast

over the keys: he looked down into the church, it was dark and still. A strange awe seized him, he felt that it was night; and the great doors locked. Hastily as his trembling limbs would allow, he crept down the stairs. Darkness shrouded the. aisles. He reached the doors, they were barred and bolted'. What would his father say? and Nanette, would she think where he was, and rouse the old door-keeper?

High up through the tower-window he caught sight of a star; and the moon poured her silver radiance full on the face of the organ. Creeping up the stairs, he once more opened the instrument. Surely some one would hear him if he played, and Nanette he knew would not leave him to stay in the old cathedral alone.

Hours passed: the full moon cast her splendor on a sweet child-face bent over

the keys in the organ-loft of the old cathedral, a smile still played about his lips, and his light brown hair lay in rings on his broad, white forehead. Franz was asleep, and while asleep he dreamed.

A beautiful lady, he thought, came to the cottage; she had a sweet, lovely face, but so sad that Franz wondered what sorrow could have come to one so rich and beautiful. The lady caught the expression of his eye, and slipping her arm around him, drew him still nearer.

"You think because I am rich that I must be happy. Learn then, my child, that wealth does not bring happiness; neither does beauty win lasting favor. To be good is to be rich, and it also makes us beautiful. The power that we have in ourselves is far superior to the outward circumstances that surround us."

"My father had this power," replied

Franz. "You see it did not profit him ;
for when he thought himself secure as
kappelmeister, the elector gave his place
to another, and now he is growing old
and blind."

"Is this so?" exclaimed the lady, a
warm light flashing into her gray eye.
"Did the elector give his place to another?"

"Indeed, he did; and it broke my
father's heart," replied Franz. "Since
then, we have neither of us known pleasure; only when we go to the cathedral,
Nanette and me; and when we return,
our father never tires of asking ques-
tions."

"This must not always be," replied
the lady. "Will you come with me, my
child, and it is possible we can show
you a way whereby you can do something for a father whom you so much
love."

"I will go with you," replied Franz; "but I must not be gone long, for my father will miss me when he wakes."

Then Franz gave his hand to the beautiful lady, and she led him by a smooth way through the most lovely wood; tall trees, filled with singing birds, skirted the banks of clear, running streams, while flowering shrubs and vines flung their perfume to the air. At length she came to a gate so strong and high Franz thought it would be impossible to open it. But as they approached, it seemed to swing back noiselessly on its hinges. Franz saw there was a lodge there, with a gray-haired man, and little children playing before the door, and as the lady passed all bowed to her.

Presently they came in sight of a magnificent castle, its walls white and glistening; while the sunlight glinting against the deep windows, flashed and

scintillated like a bed of diamonds. As
they came nearer, the lady left the broad
road, and wound along a narrow path,
and came to a little postern gate, and
up a broad marble terrace, with sparkling fountains, and with flowers brighter
than he had seen before, and birds of
gay plumage flashing their beauty through
the tree-tops. At the top of the terrace
she gave him into the care of an elderly
man, with a white flowing beard and
eyes full of tenderness. A few words
were said, and the old man took Franz
by the hand and led him into a room,
the floor of which was marble, smooth
as glass, while the walls were green and
gold. In the centre was a marble basin
or pool, with steps leading down; the
atmosphere was dim by reason of a
sweet and subtle perfume rising from
the water. Franz was hardly conscious
till he came out of the bath; then his

hair was carefully dressed, and a new
suit of clothes was brought him.

He had only time to look at himself
in the mirror, when the lady returned.
She was dressed in a rich white silk,
covered with lace and sprinkled with
pearls and diamonds.   On her head she
wore a crown; bright and sparkling as
it was, it was not half so beautiful as the
sweet face that beamed below it. The
deep traces of sorrow were gone, she
looked like one happy in the consciousness of a good deed done, and a sweet
smile was on her lip as she held out her
hand to Franz.   Together they walked
down the marble hall and up the broad
staircase, on through rows of stately ladies and martial-looking men, the crowd
opening and bowing as they passed.

At length they came to a room larger,
more magnificent than the rest.   Per-
sian carpets covered the floor, and the

windows were draped with blue and
gold. On a dais at the extremity of the
room was an oaken chair of quaint de-
vice, in which sat a proud-looking man,
pale and careworn as though weary of
so much state and ceremony.

"My child," said the prince, "Do you
feel like playing for me? I am too weak
to go to the cathedral, and I fancy if I
can hear you play I shall feel better."

Franz was a timid boy, but he loved
to please. He was always ready to play
for his father. He glanced at the lady,
there was a sweet smile resting on her
face. Dropping on his knee Franz kissed
the hand of the prince. "I will do my
best, since you are so good as to ask
me."

Franz looked up, and saw what he
had not seen before, an organ quite like
the one his father so loved.

"Play just as you do in the old cathedral," whispered the lady, and then she seated herself in a chair by the side of the prince. Franz saw nothing but the keys, he heard nothing but the sweet soul harmony, and this he must interpret to the beautiful lady and the sick prince by means of his instrument. How long he played he never knew, but when he ceased a slight hand lay on his shoulder, and a sweet face bent above him.

"To do good, Franz, is the secret of happiness. This power is yours, and so long as you use it, so long you will be happy. The dear, heavenly Father watches over and cares for those whose lives are given for the good of others." Saying this she led him away to the prince. But what was Franz's surprise! beside him on his right hand were Franz's father and mother, no longer blind, but dressed in costly robes, their faces radiant with happiness, while Nanette looked charmingly, in a white gauze dress and silver slippers. Franz was bewildered, not knowing whether to advance towards the prince, or to run and embrace his parents.

"This is the reward of obedience to your parents," said the lady, kissing the boy's white forehead.

The light of day came streaming through the tower window—the child awoke. It was cold. A chill ran through his frame. He had been in the cathedral all night, and his parents—what anguish they must have endured. Hastily as his numbed limbs would allow, he went down the stairs. A few worshippers were bowing before the altar; Franz dropped on his knees a moment, and then ran with all his speed out of the door and down the street.

Very glad were Franz's parents when

he returned, and Nanette wept for joy;
but when at breakfast he related his
dream, the face of the old organist lit up
with a great hope.

"I know, my boy, it will all come
true. So long as we love and trust Him,
the good Christ will not leave us to suffer."

Christmas had come. There were no
presents for Franz and Nanette. Only
one could they make, and this was a
nice, warm dressing-gown for their blind
father.

One day a beautiful lady took refuge
in the cottage; her carriage had broken
down, and she must stop till the postil-
ion could return to the castle. At the
cottage she heard Franz play and Nanette sing, and listened to the blind organist, as the cathedral bells broke on
the evening air.

"You must come with me," said the

lady. "We have been planning concerts at the castle, and you shall give
them."

"My children are not old enough to
go by themselves, and I am blind," replied the father.

"I will not deprive you of your children," said the lady; "my father has
influence. And besides, he has near him
an eminent physician; it is possible something can be done to restore your sight."

In three days the lady returned, and
carried Herr Hoffner with his wife and
children to the castle. Charmed with
the young musicians, the elector repent-
ed of the thoughtless deed, in depriving
the father of his position as kappelmeister. Very tenderly did he treat him now,
and under the care of the skilful physician, it was soon announced there was
hope of his recovering his sight. This
done, he was once more offered the posi-

tion; but Herr Hoffner was a just man; to do by others as he would be done by was his motto. Herr Von Stein had filled the post acceptably; it was no fault of his that the old organist had lost his place. Herr Hoffner would not accept it, but only asked that he might be allowed to give concerts with his children. Franz labored diligently at his studies, and already was he beginning to surprise his friends, not only with his playing, but with his composition.

Years passed: there was a great gathering in that grand old capital. A musical festival was in progress, and all the celebrities the world over had congregated there. Franz Hoffner was in the zenith of his glory. At the close of the performance, and while the entire audience joined in acclamations of praise to the youthful leader, a rich medal was presented. On one side the profile view of the elector and his daughter, set round with diamonds; on the other, "Music is only valuable as it lifts the heart and purifies our fallen nature."

Franz Hoffner lived to be a great musician; but he never ceased to think of his parents and Nanette. Honors were empty, and applause vain, only so far as they contributed to the happiness of those he loved.

"THE BRIDE OF THE AAR."

IT was the day after Christmas; a
heavy fall of snow during the night, the
tiny flakes full of graceful motion till
long past noon, had made a gloomy day
for the inmates of Myrtlebank. True,
there was many a gay trill and clear
silvery laugh ringing through the old
rooms. Alick was spending his college
vacation at home, and Frank and Carry
were merry as school-girls are wont to
be, when books are flung aside, and fun
and frolic take the place of study and
recitation.

"What are you dreaming about, uncle
Paul?" and Carry perched herself on
the arm of her uncle's chair, and patted
his cheek with her little dimpled hand.

"I have been thinking, child"—and there was a choking sensation in uncle Paul's throat, and a strange mist in his clear gray eyes. Carry's sympathies were awakened.

"Thinking about something long time ago, uncle Paul?" and the rosy cheek was laid close to the thin, pallid one.

"Tell us, uncle Paul; you know you promised us;" and Carry slid her arms about her uncle's neck, and felt his great heart beat against her own.

"It was a long time ago," began uncle Paul. "I had just finished my studies, and not being strong, the physician advised a year's travel on the continent. My father was a merchant, and had friends in the different European cities, and there was little danger that I should lack for attention; and with a supply of letters, and one in particular to a friend of my father's, a pastor among the mountains of Switzerland, I started. I pass over the leave-taking; finding myself alone on the sea; the nights of calm when leaning over the ship's side, looking down into the dark depths, murmuring snatches of home songs, bringing up vividly before me faces of those I loved; and as the ocean swells came rocking under us, down we went into the valleys and up over the hills of water. I felt as safe, rocked in the great cradle of the deep, as when at home. His eye was upon me; His arm encircled me.

"But pleasant as the voyage and full of memories, I see that you are impatient to pass over to the mountains of Switzerland. Words are weak to describe the magnificence of the Juras: looking upon the rolling heights shrouded with pine-trees, and down thousands of feet at the very roadside, upon cottage roofs and emerald valleys, where the deer herds were feeding quietly. All this I had seen, and then we came to a little town called Bex; and here, from too much expenditure of enthusiasm perhaps, I was confined for weeks with a raging fever.

"One day, when the fever left me weak and feeble as a child, who should enter but the good pastor Ortler. He had heard of my illness, and leaving home, he had travelled over the hills to nurse me in my weakness; and when I grew strong enough to bear it, he treated me to short drives along Lake Leman, whence we could see the meadows that skirt Geneva, the rough, shaggy mountains of Savoy, and far behind them, so far that we could not distinguish between cap and cloud, Mont Blanc and the needles of Chamouni.

"The good pastor Ortler, with his fine voice and clear, earnest eyes, was in possession at all times of a charm of manner that had for me an irresistible fascination. But when he talked of God, his greatness as seen in his works, the magnificent and matchless glory by which we were surrounded: above all, when he spoke of His tenderness and love, I realized as I had never done before the beauty of holiness, and the happiness, in this life even, of a soul firmly anchored in the faith of Christ.

"Once, I remember, he steadied my feet to a rocky point overlooking the little town of Ferney, and the deserted château of Voltaire. And then followed a conversation, in which the tenderness of the good·pastor's heart was manifest as he spoke of the fine mind wrecked on the sands of unbelief. 'And to think of this man's influence,' he said, with sorrow in his tones, and regrets over a lost life and a lost soul.

"Upon the shores of the lake stood the old home of De Stael; and nearly opposite, its white walls reflected upon the bosom of the water the house where Byron lived and wrote. In the distance we could see the gleaming roofs of Geneva, the dark cathedral, and the tall hotels. As the weeks wore on I grew stronger. Winter was coming, and the good pastor must go home. He would not hear of leaving me, and together we went down into Savoy, and over the 'mer de glâce,' and trod on the edge of frowning glaciers.

"We were sufficiently near the monastery of the great St. Bernard to take it in our path; toiling along where the ice cracked in the narrow footway, and the moon glittered on the waste of snow and glinted across the dark windows. Pastor Ortler was at home with the monks, and hardly had we thawed ourselves before the ample fireplace, when a supper was prepared, and over their well-spread tables the monks told stories of travellers lost among the granite heights, with clefts and ledges filled with ice.

"Among the rest, friar Le-Bon gave a description of the 'Ice Maiden,' or *Bride of the Aar*,' said to be seen often when the great glacier of Aar sends out icy breezes, and the echoes ring from rock to rock, as it were the audible voice of God.

"'Years ago,' he said, 'a young Englishman and his wife were travelling for scientific purposes; measuring heights, and sounding depths. They were always accompanied by guides; but now, charmed by the untold splendor, and urged by deep emotion, they climbed higher and higher, regardless of danger. Twice had the guide called out to them

that the very beauty of the day, the sun
obscured but not darkened, the softened
air, were all favorable to a snowslide or
avalanche.

"'Full of life and vivacity, the young
wife went on from one point to another, higher and higher; her lithe figure
brought out against the sky, as occasionally she plunged her iron-pointed
staff deep into the snow, and turned to
admire the vast panorama at her feet.
Her husband was making the ascent at
a slower pace, looking up to admire the
boldness of the little woman, and then
playfully scolding her as she stood poised
in mid-air so far above him. Aware of
her danger, and fearing to startle her,
the guide had ascended, and now stood
with the husband on a little ledge quite
underneath the cliff on which stood the
fearless bride.

"'A moment—there was a low, mur-

muring sound, as when the autumn leaves are swept by the evening breeze. The guide heard it, and his cheek paled. At the same time a voice was heard above.

"'"What is that, Walter, it seems as though the mountain was moving?"

"'"For heaven's sake, jump! we will catch you," shouted the guide.

"'"Quick, Gertrude!" A gleam of white shot over them, and a piercing shriek mingled with one long resounding crash, and the glittering crystal was plunged into the valley below, leaving nothing but bare jagged rocks and stunted shrubs, where all was smooth and white but a moment before. Months after, the bones of the fair English girl were buried here,' continued friar Le-Bon.

"'And her husband?' I asked.

"'They brought him here, and it was terrible to see his agony. When he grew stronger, we sent a novice with

him to England; it would not do to trust
him by himself.'

"'You do not mean to say that his
reason was gone?' I asked.

"'He was never rational after that
morning,' replied the friar; 'muttering
and moaning, and repeating the name
of Gertrude constantly. Carl left him
with his friends, and we have never
heard if he recovered.'

"'And the lady?' asked pastor Ortler.

"'On calm, still days, and just before
an avalanche,' said the kind friar, 'her
image is always seen standing upon the
loftiest height, beckoning with her white
taper fingers to some one below.'

"Entertained with so much hospital-
ity, we were loath to leave the friendly
hospice, only for the pastor's anxiety to
reach home. Down into the sweet valley of the Megringen, and northward by

Grindenwald and Thun, and up the steep heights over which falls the white foam of Reichenbach; and farther on towards the crystal Rosenlani, and the tall, still Engel Horner, we came to a little village cradled in security · beneath the towering hills; the church-spire glancing in the sunlight, and the simple cottagers jubilant in welcoming home their beloved pastor.

"At the door of the pastor's home we were met by a sweet-browed woman with a lovely infant in her arms, crowing and laughing as the father kissed it over and over again; while a boy of ten and a girl of six summers, ran with open arms to greet him.

" 'You stayed so long, papa.'

" 'And we missed you so much,' after the first greeting.

" 'This young friend was very ill; you would not have had me leave him?'

"'Oh, no, papa, but'—when the little Griselda stopped suddenly, and threw a half-defiant glance at my face, and Thorwald stood measuring me with his great black eyes.

"Hardly recovered from my illness, I stayed with the good pastor Ortler through Christmas week, and a month afterwards. Never did I pass pleasanter days. The wife Rosalind was as kind as a sister, and her children grew soon to like me as an old friend. Very simple was their manner of life, while the air they breathed was fragrant with the love they bore to Him who made and redeemed them, and who had in his good providence, set them in a pleasant place.

"Christmas to them was not a week of jubilee alone. Busy hands decorated the little church, and visits were made to the poor and sick, and presents were given without the hope of reward. Sitting by the parlor fire at night, the pastor told of the parishioners he had seen, their wants and needs; while Rosalind knit stockings, and fashioned garments.

"'It would seem that one so well fitted for society would tire of this narrow bound,' I once said. With an eye brimming over with tenderness, the pastor replied: 'There are souls to save here quite as precious as anywhere else.' I felt humbled before his quiet glance. This was the work for him to do; this was the work he loved. What matter in what part of the vineyard? wherever there was a soul. But this mountain grandeur pleased him. These quiet solitudes led him upward. The glorious diadem of the hills was always urging him onward. Hard and self-denying as his life, he had ample recompense in daily, hourly communion with the Father through the majesty of his works."

"I should like to live where I could see all this," whispered Carry.

"The heart that loves, finds beauty and grandeur everywhere." responded uncle Paul; "not only the mountain passes, but the valleys echo His praise, and there are few places so sterile but human lives abound."

"Griselda and Thorwald, have you seen them since?" asked Carry.

"Ten years afterwards, I saw them. Griselda was a tall stately girl, with blue laughing eyes, and curls of pale brown, and Thorwald was a student at Geneva. Pastor Ortler was still the same, preaching to his little flock, and giving freely of his means, his wife only slightly older. Once more we wandered over the heights and in the valleys, the spots where I lingered years before, plucking a flower and drinking from the cold glacier water. Afterward, when it became necessary for me to return, good pastor Ortler and his wife went with me, and together we passed a winter in Milan."

"And Griselda?" asked Carry.

"Oh, uncle Paul, Griselda was"— and Carry glanced up at the portrait of a young and beautiful woman hanging in a niche on the left-hand of the fire-place. Uncle Paul's portrait occupied the other side. Silence brooded over them; while to Carry it seemed the lady in the picture looked as if with recognition in her eyes. How delicate, how aerial she seemed! yet real, and true. Was it any wonder uncle Paul was so good, having had the companionship of such a spirit so many years? And as she looked, the stately frame seemed to open, and the lady to come down from her place and seat herself on the other arm of uncle Paul's chair, and to lay her head on his shoulder.

"To do good was her aim, Carry; may it be yours," said uncle Paul, and the spell was broken.

NEW BOOKS FOR THE YOUNG.

SQUARE 16MO.

Hours with Mamma. By Mrs. S. E. Dawes. Charming productions of Bible narratives, for young children, with 33 beautiful Engraving. $1 10.

Paul Venner; or the Forge and the Pulpit. A fine story, based on facts in real life, by a favorite writer for the young. The reader's liveliest interest goes with the young hero and his friends through trials and efforts which secure a noble Christian manhood. Three Engravings. $1 15.

The Hopes of Hope Castle, or Times of John Knox and Queen Mary Stuart. By Mrs. S. T. Martyn. The stirring and momentous events of the days of Knox and the bigoted Mary are here given as from the pen of a young lady of the Hope family, blending the story of home life with scenes of historical interest. A rich treasure for old and young. $1 15.

The Climbers. A grand story for boys, and their sisters too, by a new American writer. It is fitted to awaken a desire to excel in the best sense. Five Engravings. $1.

Nuts for Boys to Crack. By Rev. John Todd, D. D. Treating a variety of subjects in the pointed, shrewd, and racy style which makes this author's writings so popular and impressive. $1.

Sybil Grey; or a Year in the City. By Mrs. S. T. Martyn. A bright and charming picture from life, of a New England character, thrown amid scenes of temptation and trial, and nobly bearing the test. Sybil is a fine model for young ladies. Five fine Cuts. $1.

Grace's Visit. A choice book for young misses, displaying the power of truthfulness and Christian love to win the wayward to the Saviour. With fine Engravings. 85 cents.

Sisters, and Not Sisters. A delightful story of a sister's influence over a wayward brother. Three Cuts. $1

Lyntonville; or the Irish Boy in Canada. A fresh picture of life in the new settlements of Canada. Three Engravings. 75 cents.

Charlie Scott; or, There's Time Enough. Life on the sea-shore; the history of an orphan boy, and his battle with a bad habit. Finely illustrated. 60 cents.

Among the Willows. The blessing of self-denying efforts for the neglected. Fine Cuts. 50 cents.

Phil Kennedy. A new American tale of much interest, its facts drawn from life, and illustrating God's providential care of his people. Illustrated. 50 cents.

The Cinnamon-Isle Boy. By Mrs. E. C. Hutchings, Newark, N. J. The story of a missionary boy, Charles L. Winslow, re-told; with fresh glimpses at life in Ceylon. A true and charming narrative. Three Cuts. 60 cents.

Published and for sale by the AMERICAN TRACT SOCIETY, 150 Nassau-street, NEW YORK; 40 Cornhill, BOSTON; 1210 Chestnut-street, PHILADELPHIA; and in other cities and principal towns.

LIFE ILLUSTRATED SERIES.

Beautiful Volumes for Children.

The Weed with an Ill-name. Lessons from nature impressed upon the heart. With Cuts.

Our Village in War-Time. Thrilling life-sketches, inculcating true patriotism and piety. Illustrated.

The Swiss Children. Welcome to the little exiles from abroad. Two Cuts.

The Missing Boat. The perils of mischief, and safety of true repentance. With Cuts.

Madeline. The history of a New England girl. Illustrated.

A Little More. The value of contentment. Two Engravings.

The Lighthouse-Boy. A moral lighthouse for boys.

May Coverley. The faithful young Dress-maker. Illustrated.

Abel Grey. Raised from poverty to be a distinguished Musician. With Cuts.

Down in a Mine. Thrilling narratives of fact, illustrating the Coal-miner's mode of life, his dangers, and his security. With Engravings.

The Happy Fireside. Pleasing glimpses of home life in a model Christian household. With fine Cuts.

Kelly Nash. The boy who "did n't think." Illustrated.

Cheerily, Cheerily. An original American book, worthy of a place in every family library. Three Cuts.

While They are With Us. A series of narratives showing our duty to friends. With Engravings.

PUBLISHED AND FOR SALE BY

THE AMERICAN TRACT SOCIETY,
150 NASSAU-STREET, NEW YORK;

And for Sale at 40 Cornhill, BOSTON; 1210 Chestnut-street, PHILADELPHIA; 7 Custom-house-place, CHICAGO; and in other cities and towns.